# POLLYANNA

### ELEANOR HODGMAN PORTER

Editor: Heather Hammonds
Cover Illustration: Terry Riley
Illustrations: Terry Riley
Typesetting: Midland Typesetters

Pollyanna
First published in 2008 by
Playmore Inc., Publishers,
58 Main Street, Hackensack, N.J. 07601

Printed in China.

# The Author
## *Eleanor Hodgman Porter*
## *(1868–1920)*

American author Eleanor Hodgman Porter's character *Pollyanna* became an instant success when the book was published, in 1913. It was quickly followed by a sequel, *Pollyanna Grows Up*.

Born in New Hampshire, U.S., the young Eleanor Hodgman studied music and became a singer of some renown. She married John Porter in 1892, and gave up singing in favor of writing in the early 1900s. Her earlier books included three titles about another young girl, called *Miss Billy*.

When Eleanor Hodgman Porter died in 1920, other authors were brought in to write further stories about Pollyanna. The novel *Pollyanna* was also made into a play in 1916, and a movie in 1920. It was one of the best loved children's books of the early twentieth century.

# Contents

# Chapter 1
## *The Harrington Homestead*

The dark, dusty attic room high up in the Harrington homestead hadn't been used for years. So Nancy, who worked for Miss Polly Harrington, was most surprised when one morning, she was asked to clean it and prepare a bed.

"Nancy," said the stern-faced Miss Polly, "my eleven-year-old niece, Pollyanna, has been orphaned. I have no great love for the girl, but I have agreed that she can come and live here. The attic room will be perfectly suitable for her."

"A little girl!" cried Nancy. "Coming here, Miss Harrington? Oh, won't that be nice."

"Nice!" snapped Miss Polly. "That isn't exactly the word I'd use. However, I am not a bad woman, and I hope I know my duty."

"Of course, ma'am," replied Nancy. "I just thought a young girl might brighten things up around here; especially as you yourself live alone."

"Thank you," said Miss Harrington, "but I can't see any immediate need to brighten things up around here. I will take no pleasure in having to look after my sister's child. I see it as an irksome duty. Now hurry up Nancy, and sort the attic out."

Nancy was sorry to hear her mistress talking in such a cold way.

Miss Polly Harrington was forty years old and quite alone in the world. Her father, mother, and sister were all dead. And now Miss Polly seemed to have rejected the world, seldom being seen out. Nancy had often heard her say: "I'm not lonely. I prefer my own company. I like the peace of it."

Miss Polly had become quite used to her solitary, quiet life in the big house on the edge of the town of Beldingsfield; so used to it that she was quick to anger, even if a door banged or a spoon fell from the breakfast table.

In the little attic room, Nancy swept and scrubbed. "This is no room for a young child," she said to herself. "Hidden away alone in an attic at the top of the house. Too hot in summer and no fire in winter. What a place to put a child that's just lost her parents."

When she'd finished the room, Nancy went

"The girl can come and live here."

to see Old Tom, the gardener. "Did you know a little girl was coming to live with Miss Polly?" she asked.

"A what?" said the old man, his back creaking as he got up from where he had been kneeling and weeding. "A child! You must be joking."

"It's true," said Nancy. "Miss Polly told me herself. It's her niece."

"Well bless my soul," said Old Tom. "Young Pollyanna. I saw her once before. The sweetest girl you ever saw. And her mother, too. But I wonder what Miss Polly will do with a child in this house?"

"I wonder," said Nancy, "what a little eleven-year-old girl will do with Miss Polly!"

The old man laughed. "You ain't very fond of Miss Polly, are you?" he said.

"How could anyone be fond of her?" replied Nancy. "She's so cold."

Old Tom smiled knowingly. "I've known her for many a year and she wasn't always like she is today," he said. "You should have seen her when she was in love."

Old Tom had worked as gardener, odd job man, and driver for the Harringtons for so long that he was also the keeper of the family's secrets.

4

*"A child! You must be joking."*

"In love?" asked Nancy, who just couldn't imagine her employer in love with anyone or anything.

"Oh yes," said Tom. "Miss Polly was in love once. In love with a man who still lives in this town, even today."

"Who is he?" Nancy wanted to know.

"I'm not telling you that," replied Tom, who had served the Harrington family loyally for many years. "It ain't right that I should. But I will say this. She was in love. And she used to look right handsome. She still could if she wanted to. Miss Polly ain't really old yet. But she's been prickly ever since the love affair ended."

"Prickly," snorted Nancy. "I should say so. There's no pleasing her now."

Just then there was a call from the house. It was Miss Polly. "Nancy! Nancy!"

Nancy hurried back to the house. "I've had a telegram," said Miss Polly. "The girl's due in on the afternoon train. Get Old Tom to drive you to the station and pick her up."

"But Miss Polly," said Nancy, "surely you'd like to pick her up yourself?"

"Nonsense," replied Miss Polly. "It's not necessary at all. Now be gone with you!"

# Chapter 2
## *Pollyanna Arrives*

"I hope for Pollyanna's sake," said Nancy to Old Tom, as they drove in the horse and gig to Beldingsville station, "that the little girl doesn't drop spoons on the floor or bang doors."

"Yes," nodded Old Tom. "If she's a noisy child, I don't think much of her chances of surviving at the Harrington homestead."

The locomotive pulled into the station just as they arrived. Nancy waited until most of the passengers had got off and left the platform. Then she saw a little girl standing by herself. Wearing a red-checked gingham dress, she was a slender child with two ribboned braids of flaxen hair hanging down her back. Beneath her straw hat was a pretty and freckled face.

Pollyanna was turning to the left and right, plainly looking for someone. Nancy knew at once that it was the girl she was looking for.

Nancy walked over to the child. "You must be Pollyanna," she said.

"Oh I am," Pollyanna replied. "And I'm so glad, glad, glad to see you. I'd hoped you'd come to meet me."

"You did?" asked Nancy, rather puzzled that the girl addressed her as if she knew who she was.

"Yes," said Pollyanna. "I was wondering what you would look like. And now I know. And I'm just very glad that you look just how you look."

Old Tom put the girl's trunk on the buggy and the three of them set off back to Miss Polly's.

"Oh, I'm so glad," said Pollyanna as they drove through the countryside. "I'm so glad it's pretty here. I knew it would be. What could be nicer; pretty countryside and an aunt who's come to pick me up."

Nancy suddenly realized the mistake the girl had made. "Oh, but I'm not your aunt," she said. "I'm not your Aunt Polly."

"You aren't?" said Pollyanna, with a very surprised look on her face.

"No," she said, shaking her head. "I'm only Nancy. I work for your aunt. And this gentleman here is Old Tom, the gardener."

"Oh well," smiled the girl. "That's even better then. I've already met you both and that

*Pollyanna was plainly looking for someone.*

was nice, and I've still got the pleasure to come of meeting Miss Polly."

Both Nancy and Old Tom smiled at the child's view of the situation.

"Is my aunt rich?" asked Pollyanna. "Does she live in a big house? I can't remember because I only came here once when I was very young."

"Oh yes, she's rich," said Nancy. "And she does live in a big house."

"I'm so glad," said Pollyanna. "I expect she has carpets in all the rooms and eats ice cream every afternoon. I do hope so."

"Sadly," said Nancy, "I don't think your aunt likes ice creams."

"How could anybody not like ice creams!" exclaimed Pollyanna. "Then, what about carpets?"

"Yes, your aunt does have carpets in most rooms," said Nancy, but quickly remembered the attic room. "Though not all the rooms have carpets."

"And are there pictures on the walls?" the little girl wanted to know.

Nancy didn't have time to answer. They had reached the Harrington homestead.

There was no sign of Miss Polly waiting

*"I'm so glad it's pretty here."*

outside the house to welcome her niece. That didn't surprise Nancy at all. If she couldn't be bothered to pick the child up from the station, she wouldn't take the time to meet her at the front door. Instead, Old Tom unloaded the girl's trunk and the three went into the house.

It was dark inside. Miss Polly had asked specifically that day for the curtains to be drawn to keep out the sunshine.

"It's going to be fun having you to stay here," said Old Tom. "We need to have some young blood in the house."

"Oh you can't imagine how glad I am to be here," said Pollyanna. "Everything's so new and exciting."

At that moment, Miss Polly's voice rang out from the parlor. "Is that you Nancy? Bring the girl in right away."

# Chapter 3
## *The Attic*

Miss Polly Harrington was sitting in her comfortable armchair, reading a book. She did not rise to meet her niece, although she did manage to look up from her book and hold out a limp hand to be shaken.

"How do you do, Pollyanna," she said.

There was no time for her to say another word, for Pollyanna fairly flew across the room and flung herself into Miss Polly's unwelcoming lap.

"Oh, Aunt Polly," she cried, "you don't know how glad I am that you've let me come to stay with you! It will be perfectly lovely to live with you and Nancy, and Old Tom."

"That will do, my girl!" replied Miss Polly sharply, as she tried to unlock the arms now encircling her affectionately. "A handshake is enough. You mustn't be so affectionate."

Miss Polly finally freed herself from the little girl. Pollyanna didn't know what to think. There were tears in her eyes. The poor child had been hurt by Miss Polly's chill greeting.

"Now," said Miss Polly, "I will show you your room. I hope Old Tom has already taken up your trunk. Follow me."

Without speaking, Pollyanna followed her aunt out of the room and up the long staircase. She stared at the beautiful stair carpet, and the even more colorful carpet on the landing at the top of the stairs.

"What a lovely house you have, Aunt," she said. "How awfully glad you must be to live here. You must also be glad you're so rich."

"I don't care to talk of money," replied Miss Polly, who was already thinking how lucky it was that she had decided to put the girl in the attic, where she couldn't be heard or seen too often.

Meanwhile, Pollyanna was wondering which of the lovely rooms she would be put in. Then Miss Polly opened the door to the attic stairs and began climbing the bare wooden steps . . .

Pollyanna's dreams of plush carpets and finely decorated rooms began to fade. But the thought still lingered that her room would be beautiful, with colorful curtains, carpets, rugs, and lovely pictures.

14

*Pollyanna fairly flew across the room.*

At the top of the dimly lit stairs, Pollyanna saw stacks of old trunks and boxes. And behind them was a rough door. Her aunt threw it open.

"There, Pollyanna," she said. "Here is your room. I see your trunk is here, so you can unpack now. I'll send up Nancy to help you. Supper is at six."

If Pollyanna's dreams of living in a beautiful room were shattered, she didn't show it. "My father would have loved to have lived here," she said, "but he's gone to heaven to join my mother. I shall think lots about them when I'm here. They'll know I'm safe, now that I have you to look after me."

Miss Polly didn't know what to say. "Pollyanna," she said at last, "there is one thing that you must understand right away. I do not care to have you keep talking about your father and mother."

Miss Polly would have reason to remember those words in times to come.

Pollyanna's aunt swept out of the room and shut the door behind her. She could be heard clunking hastily down the hard wooden stairs.

The little girl looked around her, staring

*"Here is your room."*

at the bare walls, the bare floor, and the bare windows. Then she looked at her trunk, the last remnant of her past life. She fell on her knees at its side, covered her face with her hands, and began to cry.

Nancy found her still on her knees when she came up a few minutes later. "Oh you poor dear," she said. "My poor little lamb. I knew you would feel like this."

Pollyanna cried all the harder, and buried herself in Nancy's arms. "Why did my mother die? Why did my father pass away? Why did they have to go?"

Nancy kept her tight in her arms for several minutes. "Now my little sweet," she said after a while, "let's unpack the trunk."

"There isn't much to unpack," wept Pollyanna. "I've only a dress or two."

Suddenly, she cheered up. "Why," she said, "I'm glad I only have two dresses. It won't take us long to unpack the trunk, will it?"

For the first time, Nancy saw how Pollyanna saw the good things in life, however bleak the outlook was. It certainly wasn't going to be the last time, either.

A few minutes later, Pollyanna looked out at the view from the window. "Isn't it beautiful,"

*Pollyanna buried herself in Nancy's arms.*

she sighed. "Just look at those tall trees, the pretty houses, and the lovely church. And the river is truly shining in the sun. Who needs pictures in a room when the picture outside is so beautiful. Oh, I'm so glad now that I have this room."

Nancy, much to Pollyanna's surprise, burst into tears!

# Chapter 4
## *Out of the Window!*

When Nancy had gone downstairs to prepare supper, Pollyanna decided to try and open the window. She undid the latch and it opened easily. Fresh air rushed into the tiny attic, filling it with the smells of summer. A big fly swept past her nose and buzzed happily around the room.

Then Pollyanna noticed something very exciting indeed. Just outside the window was a tree with its branches grown tall and wide. Suddenly, she laughed out aloud. "I can't believe it. What luck!"

The little girl climbed nimbly onto the window ledge. From there, it was an easy matter to step onto the nearest branch of the tree. Then, clinging like a monkey, she swung herself from branch to branch, until the lowest branch was reached. It was still a long drop to the ground, even for Pollyanna. But she swung herself into the air and landed in the soft grass below.

*She swung herself from branch to branch.*

Pollyanna picked herself up and looked eagerly around. She was at the back of the house and before her lay a garden, where Old Tom the gardener was working. Beyond the garden was a path leading up a steep hill, at the top of which a lone pine tree stood guard beside a large rock.

To Pollyanna, at that moment, there was only one place she wanted to be . . . on top of that rock!

With a run and a skillful turn, Pollyanna skipped by Old Tom, threaded her way neatly between the rows of sweet peas, and reached the path. From the window of her room, the rock had looked so near. Now, from the ground, it looked miles away.

\*\*\*

Fifteen minutes later the great clock in the hallway of the Harrington homestead struck six o'clock. At precisely the last stroke, Nancy sounded the bell for supper.

One, two, three minutes passed. Miss Polly, who had already taken her seat at the dining room table, frowned and tapped her foot impatiently.

"Nancy," she said, "my niece is late."

Nancy made a move toward the door. She was going to get Pollyanna.

"No," said Miss Polly. "You need not call her. I told her what time supper was and now she will have to suffer the consequences. She may as well learn right now to be punctual. If she finally comes down, she may have bread and milk in the kitchen. But that's all."

"Bread and milk!" muttered Nancy to herself as she left the room and climbed to the attic. "The poor child's just been crying her heart out. She'll need more than bread and milk tonight."

Nancy was puffing by the time she got all the way up to the attic room. It was, of course, empty. "Where are you child?" she called out. "Where've you gone?"

She flew downstairs and out into the garden, where she bumped into Old Tom. "The blessed child's gone," she cried. "She's vanished right up into heaven, I'm sure."

"Well," said Old Tom. "She might have tried to get to heaven, and that's a fact. But I don't think she got far enough."

Old Tom pointed with his crooked finger to the rock on top of the hill where the evening

*Old Tom pointed to the young girl.*

sky now sharply outlined the wind-blown figure of a young girl. Nancy was off again, breaking into a run as she approached the hill. She was almost out of breath again when she reached the top, and caught sight of Pollyanna as she slid down the rock.

"I was so scared. I thought I'd lost you," scolded Nancy.

"Oh, I'm sorry Nancy," said Pollyanna, getting up from the ground and rubbing the dirt off her clothes. "Don't ever get scared because of me. I always come back all right."

"But I didn't even see you go," said Nancy. "I guess you must have flown through the roof."

"I did fly," laughed Pollyanna. "But not up through the roof. I flew down the tree outside my window."

"My goodness," gasped Nancy. "I'd like to know what your aunt would say about that. You could have fallen to your death."

"Well I'll tell her," smiled Pollyanna. "Then you'll find out what she would say."

Oh, how her cheery words made Nancy laugh!

# Chapter 5
## *The Game*

Nancy knew Pollyanna was hungry after her expedition. But she had to obey her mistress's orders. "Your aunt was angry that you didn't turn up to supper on time," she said. "So I'm afraid you'll have to have bread and milk with me in the kitchen."

"That makes me glad," said Pollyanna, using her favorite word again. "I love bread and milk. I'd love to have it with you in your kitchen."

"You're a funny little thing," said Nancy. "You always seem glad about everything . . . your room, the view, bread and milk. Everything makes you glad."

"Well that's the game, you know," smiled Pollyanna.

"What do you mean, the game?"

"We used to call it our 'just being glad' game," explained Pollyanna.

Nancy was even more confused. "What in the world are you talking about?"

"It was my father's game," she replied. "We played it ever since I was a little girl. We played it all the time."

"What sort of game is it?" asked Nancy.

"Well," said Pollyanna, "it's a game about always trying to find something to be glad about, however miserable or sad we might be. It all started with a pair of crutches. My father had ordered me a new doll for Christmas and by mistake the shop sent me crutches instead."

"Crutches," said Nancy. "They're good to help people walk, but there's nothing glad about crutches."

"That's what we thought at first," said Pollyanna. "Then Father thought of something glad about them first, and then I came up with the same idea too."

"Well, suppose you tell me," smiled Nancy, "what made you glad about the crutches?"

"Easy," said Pollyanna. "My father and I were just glad that we didn't need them."

"Well I'll be blowed," said Nancy. "I understand now."

"We always played the game after that," said Pollyanna. "And the harder it was to see something glad, the better the game."

"But what about your attic room?" asked Nancy. "It's so plain and uncomfortable. Why are you glad about that?"

"That was a hard one at first," said Pollyanna. "I was so lonesome that I just didn't feel like playing the game. Then I saw the lovely view from the window. And better than that, I saw there was no mirror in the room."

"What's good and glad about not having a mirror?" asked Nancy.

"If there isn't a mirror, then it means I can't see my freckles," she replied. "And I hate my freckles. So I'm very glad that I have no mirror!"

Nancy burst into tears again, but this time they were tears of laughter.

"Generally," said Pollyanna, "it doesn't take long to find something to be glad about. Maybe Aunt Polly will play the game with me sometime. I'd be really glad if she does."

"I'm not so sure about your aunt," said Nancy, "and I ain't saying I'll play the game well either. But I'll play it with you and see how I get on."

Pollyanna was so glad that Nancy wanted to play the game. "We'll have such fun," she said.

*"We used to call it our 'just being glad' game."*

After having her bread and milk, Nancy suggested that Pollyanna should go and see her aunt. So Pollyanna went into the parlor, where Miss Polly was reading.

"Have you had your supper?" her aunt asked.

"Yes, Aunt Polly," she replied.

"You must remember to be on time for supper," said Miss Polly sternly. "The bread and milk was your punishment."

"But I was very glad to get it," said Pollyanna. "I like bread and milk. So don't feel bad about giving me that for supper."

Miss Polly suddenly sat up straight in her chair. What the girl had said had quite surprised her.

"Right, Pollyanna," she said. "It's time you were in bed. Tomorrow we must plan what you are going to do and how long you are going to spend on everything. Keep to a timetable and you won't get into trouble like you did tonight. Breakfast is at half past seven. Make sure you're down on time."

Pollyanna gave her aunt an affectionate hug. "I've had such a happy time here so far," she said. "I know I'm just going to love living with you. Goodnight."

*"The bread and milk was your punishment."*

"Upon my soul!" said Miss Polly to herself after Pollyanna had gone to bed. "What an extraordinary girl. How could anyone be glad that I punished them?"

But upstairs in the attic, the little girl was finding it hard to find something glad about sleeping in a lonely room.

"I might feel better about things if I was sleeping near Nancy or Aunt Polly, rather than alone way up here in a dark attic," she whispered sadly.

# Chapter 6
## *All Work and No Play*

Pollyanna woke early the next day. Outside, the sun was shining in a bright blue sky.

The attic was cooler now and the air blew in fresh and sweet. The birds were twittering joyously in the tree, and Pollyanna ran to the window to talk to them.

She looked out of the window and saw that Aunt Polly was already outside, trimming the roses with Old Tom. Then she quickly dressed, rushed down the attic stairs, crossed the landing, hurtled down the main staircase, and ran straight out of the front door and into the garden.

She spotted Aunt Polly, and laughing with delight, flung herself upon her.

"Oh, Aunt Polly," she said. "I reckon I'm glad just to be alive this morning."

"Pollyanna!" said the lady very sternly. "Is this the usual way you say good morning?"

The happy girl dropped to her toes and danced lightly up and down. "No," she said.

"Only when I love folks. I just wanted to hug you."

Miss Polly tried to frown, but didn't really succeed too well. She soon left Pollyanna alone with Old Tom.

"I'm so glad to see you again, Mr. Tom," said Pollyanna.

"I'm glad to see you too, child," the old man smiled. "You are so like your mother. I used to know her when she was about the same age as you are now. She was a right little Miss, too. You see, I've been working in this garden for longer than I care to remember."

Pollyanna caught her breath. She was so surprised at what Old Tom had just said. "You really knew my mother? Oh please tell me about her."

Pollyanna plumped herself down in the middle of the dirt, put her elbows on her knees and looked up, waiting for Old Tom to begin. But the very next moment, she heard a bell ring and saw Nancy flying out of the door toward her.

"Hurry up, Miss Pollyanna," she panted. "The bell means it's breakfast time. We don't want you getting into trouble with Miss Polly again, do we."

*She flung herself upon Aunt Polly.*

Then she shooed Pollyanna back into the house, just like an old maid might shoo a chicken into its shed.

After breakfast, Miss Polly announced that Pollyanna would be going to school in the fall. "And until then," she said, "you will do your lessons under my guidance."

She then gave Pollyanna a rundown of her weekly tasks. "You will clean your bedroom before breakfast. You will read to me for a half an hour every morning at nine o'clock, except on Sundays. You will spend the rest of the morning on Wednesdays and Saturdays with Nancy, learning to cook. On all other mornings except Sundays, I shall teach you to sew. And during the afternoons you will learn to play the piano."

Pollyanna cried out in dismay. "Oh, but Aunt Polly, you haven't left me any time just . . . to live."

"To live, child!" exclaimed Aunt Polly. "What do you mean? You're living all the time."

"Of course, I'm breathing all the time," said Pollyanna. "But that doesn't necessarily mean I am living and doing things. You breathe when you sleep, but you aren't living. I mean

*Shooing Pollyanna back into the house.*

living as in playing outdoors, reading to myself, climbing hills, and talking to Mr. Tom in the garden. That's what I call living. Aunt Polly, living isn't just breathing."

Miss Polly lifted her head irritably. "Pollyanna, you really are the most extraordinary girl. Of course, you will be allowed a certain amount of play time. But it seems to me that if I am going to do my duty to you, then you ought to be willing to do yours by not wasting the education I shall give you."

Pollyanna looked shocked. "I could never be ungrateful to you, Aunt Polly. Why, I love you. And you are my only aunt!"

"Very well," said Miss Polly. "I hope you mean what you say, child."

That night, Pollyanna tried very hard to be glad about something. At last something came to mind. "How glad I will be when all my lessons and other duties are done," she said to herself.

# Chapter 7
## *A Rooftop Adventure*

The next day Pollyanna spent a happy morning learning to cook with Nancy. In the afternoon she had piano practice. Afterwards, she ran out into the garden to look for Old Tom. She found him in the vegetable garden. "Oh do tell me about my mother," she begged.

Old Tom spent the next hour talking about Pollyanna's mother and what she was like as a child. It seemed to Pollyanna that her mother was always getting into trouble.

"As I said," Old Tom laughed, "she was probably as mischievous as you are."

That night when Pollyanna went to bed, she couldn't sleep because it was so hot. "If only my bed was out of doors," she thought.

Then an idea struck her. She took a blanket and a pillow, and climbed out of her window. Then, climbing down over the roof, she reached a gully. She laid out the blanket and pillow, and settled down to sleep in the cool of the night air.

*Sleeping in the cool of the night air.*

What Pollyanna didn't realize was that she had chosen a place on the roof immediately above Aunt Polly's room. And what she didn't hear was her aunt leaping out of bed and calling for Old Tom.

"Quick," she said. "Come right away. Somebody's on the roof. It must be a burglar. Hurry! Quick!"

A few minutes later, Pollyanna awoke to see the top of a ladder just beside her. And peering from the top of it was Old Tom. "So you're the burglar," he laughed.

"What does this mean?" roared Aunt Polly, when she discovered that her niece was the culprit.

Pollyanna rubbed her eyes sleepily. "It was so hot that I decided to sleep outside," she explained.

"What can I say," said Aunt Polly. "You will sleep with me in my bedroom for the rest of the night, so I can keep an eye on you."

"Me? Sleep with you in your bedroom?" said Pollyanna. "How wonderful. How perfectly lovely of you! You can't imagine how glad I would be to sleep in your room."

Miss Polly was speechless. It seemed that each time she wanted to punish Pollyanna, the

*"You will sleep with me in my bedroom."*

child was just grateful for whatever punishment she gave her!

She was feeling curiously helpless, and didn't know what to think. And the longer she knew Pollyanna, the more that mood continued to grow inside her.

\*\*\*

42

Life at the Harrington homestead settled down into something like a normal order in the following days, though not exactly the order that Miss Polly had wanted.

Somehow, Pollyanna found plenty of time to live as well as learn her lessons. She also spent time visiting the town of Beldingsfield. She loved meeting strangers and getting to know them.

It was on one of those excursions that she met "The Man". In the days that followed, she often saw him out on walks. The Man always wore a long black coat and a high silk hat. His hair was rather gray. He walked erect and rather speedily, and he was always alone.

Pollyanna felt vaguely sorry for him. Perhaps that was why one afternoon she gathered up her courage and spoke to him.

# Chapter 8
## *The Man*

"How do you do, sir?" Pollyanna said to The Man. "Isn't this a lovely day?"

The Man stopped and stared at her with surprise. "Did you speak to me?" he asked in a sharp voice.

"Yes, sir," she replied. "It's a nice day, isn't it?"

"Eh? Oh! Humph!" he grunted, and strode on again.

Pollyanna laughed. He was such a funny man, she thought.

The next day she saw him again. "It isn't quite as nice as yesterday, is it?" she said.

The Man answered as he had the day before. "Eh? Oh! Humph!"

The next day she approached him a third time.

"See here, child," he said. "Who are you? And why are you speaking to me every day?"

"I thought you looked lonely," she said. "I'm so glad you stopped. Now we can be properly

*"My name is Pollyanna. What's yours?"*

introduced. My name is Pollyanna. What's
yours?"

"Well, of all the cheek!" said The Man,
walking on faster than ever.

It was raining the next time Pollyanna saw
him. "The weather isn't so nice today, is it,
sir?" she said.

The Man did not even grunt this time, but
hurried on. She thought he might not have
heard her. So the next time they met, she spoke
up much louder.

"How do you do?" she chirped. "I'm so glad
it isn't yesterday. The weather was much worse
then. What do you think, sir?"

The Man stopped abruptly. "Listen to me,
young lady," he said. "I've got other things
beside the weather to think of. I never know
whether the sun shines or not. Why don't you
find someone of your own age to talk to?"

"I'd like to," she said, "but there don't seem
to be many children about. Anyway, I like old
folks."

The next day they met again. This time
The Man spoke first. "Good afternoon," he
said rather stiffly. "Perhaps I had better say
right away that I know that the sun is shining
today."

"You don't have to tell me," said Pollyanna. "I knew you knew, as soon as I saw your
smile."

"Oh, you did, did you?" he replied.

The Man always spoke to Pollyanna after
that. One day Nancy was with Pollyanna when
she waved at The Man, and he said what a nice
day it was.

"Good grief," said Nancy in a shaky voice.
"Did that man speak to you?"

"Why yes," replied Pollyanna. "We talk
every day."

"Do you know who he is?" she asked.

Pollyanna shook her head. "I reckon he
forgot to introduce himself. But I told him my
name."

Nancy shook head in a puzzled way. "That
man hasn't spoken to anyone in years," she
said. "His name is John Pendleton. He lives all
by himself, and he's really rich. Some say he's
crazy. Others say he has a skeleton in his cupboard. He's a great mystery."

Pollyanna was wondering just then why a
man would keep a skeleton in a cupboard.
She was so young she didn't understand that it
was just a phrase meaning that someone had a
secret hidden away.

*Pollyanna waved at The Man.*

## The Man

"I truly believe," said Nancy, "that you're the first person I have ever seen him talk to."

There was only one answer Pollyanna could give to that. "I'm glad," she said.

# Chapter 9
## A New Room for Pollyanna

One day Aunt Polly went up into the attic to find an old shawl she had put away into storage. Absent mindedly, she wandered into Pollyanna's room. The girl was sitting alone on a straight-backed chair.

"Oh, how lovely to see you," said Pollyanna. "I love company. I don't get many visitors up here, but I do like my room. It's the first real room I have had in my life. It does belong to me, doesn't it?"

"Why, yes," said Miss Polly. "I suppose it does."

"Yes, I love this room," Pollyanna continued, "even if it hasn't got carpets, curtains, and pictures, which I would have loved to . . ."

Pollyanna stopped in mid-sentence, as if she was frightened to say what she wanted.

"Go on," said Miss Polly, sitting on the edge of Pollyanna's bed. "Finish what you wanted to say."

"It's nothing really," she sighed, "but I'd

*Talking with Pollyanna, in her room.*

been kind of planning on pretty carpets and lace curtains, and things like that."

"Planning on them," interrupted Miss Polly sharply.

"I ought not to have planned," said Pollyanna. "It was only because I had never had them in my life before."

Miss Polly rose to her feet. "That will be enough," she said. "You have said quite enough, I am sure."

The next minute she swept out of the room and vanished down the stairs. But something very strange happened, soon after. Miss Polly gave orders to Nancy to move all Pollyanna's things to the room next to hers, on the first floor.

"I have decided that my niece should sleep there for the present," she said.

"Yes, ma'am," said Nancy out aloud.

"Oh, glory be," she thought to herself.

"You won't believe this," she said to Pollyanna a short time later. "The mistress of Harrington homestead has given you a new bedroom—the one right besides hers!"

"Are you sure?" asked Pollyanna, hardly able to believe what she had heard.

"Well, she's told me to move all your things downstairs," said Nancy. "So that's what I'm going to do, and quickly in case she changes her mind."

Pollyanna raced downstairs and into the parlor where Miss Polly was sitting reading a book, as usual. The young girl leapt into her aunt's lap once again.

"Do you mean it?" she said excitedly. "Am I to move downstairs into a lovely room beside yours? I know the room. It has carpets, curtains, and lots of lovely pictures on the walls. I shall be so happy . . . so glad."

*"She's told me to move all your things downstairs."*

"Now, there's no reason to get so excited about it all," said Miss Polly. "I'm pleased you like the change, but make sure you take care of everything in the room, Pollyanna."

Miss Polly looked at the expression of joy on Pollyanna's face, and for some inexplicable reason, felt like crying. In fact, a tear did come to her eye, but she didn't let Pollyanna see it. "Just make sure you don't go banging the doors," she said, "because you are right beside my room."

"I shall never bang another door in my life," said Pollyanna. "I shall be as quiet as a mouse."

"I should hope so," said Miss Polly.

"And will you be glad if I don't bang doors, Aunt?" asked Pollyanna.

"I will be truly glad," was the reply.

That made Pollyanna very glad indeed. She was beginning to think that Miss Polly didn't know how to be glad. "And that would be such a terrible shame," thought the girl.

What Pollyanna didn't know was that once upon a time, Miss Polly had been very glad about a lot of things. Old Tom knew that.

# Chapter 10
## *A Kitten, a Dog, and a Little Boy*

Midsummer brought more arrivals at the Harrington homestead. The first was a kitten.

Pollyanna found it mewing pitifully, just down the road from the house. She tried unsuccessfully to find out if anyone owned it, and then brought it home.

"I was glad it didn't belong to anyone," she told her aunt, "because I wanted to bring it home. I love kittens. I knew you'd be glad to let it live here."

Miss Polly looked at the sad little creature in Pollyanna's arms and shivered. She hated cats. "Ugh!" she said. "What a dirty little beast! It's sick, I'm sure. And it's all mangy, and full of fleas."

"I know it's a poor little thing," said Pollyanna. "It's so scared that it's trembling. You see, it doesn't know yet that we're going to keep it."

"No, nor does anybody else," replied Miss Polly, who had no intention of letting the kitten stay.

"I've told everyone we're going to keep it," said Pollyanna. "I knew you'd be glad to have it, poor little lonesome thing. I've called it Fluffy."

Miss Polly opened her lips and tried to speak. But no words came out. The curious helpless feeling that had been hers so often since Pollyanna's arrival had taken a good hold on her. She tried to fight it. "Pollyanna," she said, "I don't really want to have a . . ."

But Pollyanna was already on her way to the kitchen, to speak to Nancy. "Look," she said, rushing in to the kitchen with the kitten. "Aunt Polly has two children to bring up now; the kitten and me!"

The next day, Pollyanna brought back a homeless dog, even dirtier and sadder-looking than the kitten. Once more, Miss Polly was unable to turn it away. Pollyanna named it Buffy.

The following day Pollyanna saw a small, ragged boy sitting by the roadside. He looked so sad and lonely that she went across to speak to him.

*Pollyanna found a kitten.*

57

"My name's Pollyanna," she said. "What's yours?"

"Jimmy Bean," he grunted ungraciously.

"And where do you live?"

"Nowhere," said the boy.

"Nowhere?" said Pollyanna. "Everybody lives somewhere."

"Well, I don't, you silly girl," he grumbled.

Pollyanna tossed her head a little. She didn't like to be called silly.

"So where did you used to live?" she asked.

"Well, if that don't beat everything for asking questions," he said.

"I have to ask such questions," she replied haughtily, "or else I won't find out about you."

The boy gave a short laugh. "All right then," he said, "here goes. I'm Jimmy Bean. I'm ten years old. I came here to live in the orphans' home, but they had so many kids, there wasn't room for me. So I ain't wanted anywhere. Yes, I'd like a home—one with a mother in it."

Pollyanna suddenly began to feel glad. She knew who would look after the boy . . . Miss Polly. "My aunt would take you in," she smiled. "She's like a mother to me, and I'm an orphan too."

*The boy looked so sad and lonely.*

"Would she?" said Jimmy. "I'm a hard worker and I'm real strong."

He bared a small bony arm to prove it.

"Of course, she'd take you in," insisted Pollyanna, tugging at his arm. "Come on. My Aunt Polly is the nicest lady in the world. And she has rooms! Heaps of them! Maybe you'll have to start off in the attic. I did at first. You'll love it."

When they reached the house, the boy was pushed straight into the presence of a very surprised Aunt Polly.

"Dear Aunt," said Pollyanna. "Just look here, I've found something else you can bring up. It's much nicer than even Fluffy and Buffy. It's a real live little boy. He won't mind a bit sleeping in the attic at first and he says he can work hard, but I'll need him most of the time to play with, I reckon."

Miss Polly went white, then very red. "And who is this dirty little boy? Where on earth did you find him?" she asked, feeling rather faint.

# Chapter 11
## *Jimmy Bean*

"This is Jimmy Bean, Aunt," Pollyanna announced happily.

"And what is he doing here?" Miss Polly asked, getting out of her chair.

"Why, Aunt, I just told you. He's for you. I brought him for you. There's no room in the orphanage, so I said he could come to you. I know he's very dirty, but washed up he'll be even nicer than Fluffy or Buffy."

Miss Polly dropped back into her chair, and raised a shaking hand to her throat. The old helplessness was threatening once more to overcome her. Then, with a visible struggle, she suddenly pulled herself erect.

"That will do, Pollyanna," she said. "This is the most absurd thing you have done yet. As if scrawny cats and dogs weren't bad enough, now you bring home ragged little beggars off the street."

The boy stirred. "I ain't a beggar, ma'am,"

he said, "and I don't want nothing from you. I would work to pay for my bed. In any case, I wasn't coming to bother you until the girl told me how kind and nice you were, and just dying to help boys like me. So there!"

Without another word, the boy turned around and marched out of the room.

"Oh Aunt Polly," cried Pollyanna. "I was sure you'd be glad to have him here. I should think you'd be glad . . ."

Miss Polly raised her hand. "Stop! Don't mention that word again. I will not be very glad to hear it again. All I get from you is 'glad' from morning till night. I think you will drive me mad with the word!"

Pollyanna was shocked. Her jaw dropped from sheer amazement at her aunt's anger. She thought about telling her what the glad game was. But she didn't because it was her father's game, and Miss Polly had made it quite clear that she didn't want to hear Pollyanna talk about her father.

"I thought you would have been gl. . . Oh!"

Pollyanna broke off, clapping a hand over her mouth to stop the word from coming out, and then she hurried off to find the boy.

She soon caught up with him. "I'm so sorry,"

*The boy marched out of the room.*

she said. "I thought my aunt would have behaved very differently."

"I don't blame you," he replied. "But I ain't no beggar. I have my pride. And I won't be spoken to like that."

"Of course not," said Pollyanna. "But don't worry about all this. I know Aunt would love to look after you. It's just that she doesn't know it yet. But she will."

***

That afternoon Pollyanna was walking in the woods near the town when she heard a dog barking. The dog sounded most alarmed. Pollyanna ran to where the sound was coming from. Suddenly, the dog ran out into the path in front of her. Whining and whimpering, it seemed to be telling her to follow. Its tail was quivering.

Pollyanna followed the dog. It led her straight to a man, who was lying motionless at the foot of an overhanging rock beside the path. It was "The Man", or John Pendleton as she now knew him to be. He started to move as she reached him.

"Mr. Pendleton, are you hurt?" she asked.

"What do you think?" he snapped. "Do

*"Mr. Pendleton, are you hurt?"*

you think I'm just taking a rest in the sun? Of course I'm hurt. Go and telephone Doctor Chilton. Tell him to come quickly, and to bring two men and a stretcher. I've broken my leg."

Pollyanna ran off home immediately. She met Nancy and told her what had happened. "He wants us to telephone Doctor Chilton for him," she said.

Nancy promised to telephone and Pollyanna explained where the man could be found, before rushing out of the house and running all the way back.

Mr. Pendleton was still lying on the path, and still in great pain.

"The doctor will be here soon," she said, kneeling down beside him.

The dog sat quietly nearby, satisfied that its master was being cared for.

# Chapter 12
## *Nurse Pollyanna*

Ever since Pollyanna had first met Mr. Pendleton, he'd always been rather gruff and short with her. To most people, he would have appeared very rude indeed. Yet Pollyanna seemed to understand him.

"I thought you wouldn't come back," he said.

"Of course I came back," she answered. "I didn't want to leave you alone. I wanted to be with you."

"I think you might have found a more pleasant companion to spend your time with," he said.

"Why do you say that?" she asked. "Is it because you always seem cross when you see me?"

"Yes," he said, "I am cross a lot. I'm sorry."

"You are cross outside yourself," she said. "But inside you aren't cross a bit."

"And how do you know that?" he asked.

"I can tell from your dog," she said.

Mr. Pendleton's dog was now resting its head on his chest. And his arm was curled affectionately around the animal's neck.

"It's funny how dogs and cats know what's going on inside their owners' minds better than other human beings," she said.

The man smiled knowingly, even though he was in great pain. Pollyanna held his hand in hers. At last the dog pricked up its ears and began to whine. The next moment the doctor and two helpers arrived with a stretcher.

"Well, you've been playing nurse, have you?" said Doctor Chilton, who knew of the young girl.

"A little," she said. "I'm glad I was here."

"So am I," said the doctor. "I've no doubt you have helped him."

Then Mr. Pendleton was put on the stretcher and carried away.

Pollyanna was late back for supper that day and she was worried that her aunt would be angry with her. But on getting home, Nancy explained that Miss Polly had been called away to visit a sick friend. "She'll be away for three days," said Nancy. "We'll be looking after ourselves until then."

"I don't want to say I'm glad someone's ill,"

*The doctor and two helpers arrrived.*

said Pollyanna. "But it will be fun with just the two of us and Old Tom . . . and Fluffy and Buffy, of course."

\*\*\*

When Miss Polly returned, Pollyanna told her all about the accident and how John Pendleton had broken his leg.

Miss Polly almost sprang from her chair, "John Pendleton!" she cried.

"That's his name," replied Pollyanna.

"Do you really know him?" asked Miss Polly.

"Yes," she said. "He speaks to me sometimes. He's really quite a nice man, and I'd like to take him some jelly to cheer him up."

"I doubt you'd ever cheer him up," said Miss Polly. "He's lived alone for years. And he hardly ever speaks a word to anyone."

The next day Pollyanna walked around to Mr. Pendleton's house. She was met by Doctor Chilton, who was visiting his patient.

"I've brought Mr. Pendleton some jelly," she explained.

"Oh, I'm sure he'll like that," replied the doctor.

*"I've brought Mr. Pendleton some jelly."*

The doctor led Pollyanna to a room at the back of the house. They were about to enter when a nurse came out.

"Doctor," she said, "please remember that Mr. Pendleton has given orders not to admit anyone."

"Yes, but I'm giving the orders now," the doctor replied. "This young lady will be a tonic to him. If anyone can cheer him up, she will."

"And what sort of tonic is that?" asked the nurse.

"An overwhelming and unquenchable gladness for everything that has happened, or is going to happen," said the doctor. "I hear from my patients that Pollyanna sees gladness in everything. I only wish I could give her to all my patients as a tonic."

So Pollyanna was led into Mr. Pendleton's bedroom.

"I said that no one was to be allowed in to see me," he said, when he spotted someone at his door. Then he saw who it was.

"Oh, it's you, is it?" he said. "Why are you here?"

"I have brought you some jelly," Pollyanna replied. "I thought it might take your mind off your broken leg."

"I never eat jelly!" he snapped.

"Then you can have your first jelly today," she insisted.

"Jelly will not cure me," said Mr. Pendleton. "I shall lie in this bed forever."

"You should be glad you didn't break both your legs," she said.

"That's like saying a centipede should be grateful if it only broke fifty of its one hundred legs," he said. "I expect you would say that I should be glad the doctor is here and glad that I have a nurse to look after me."

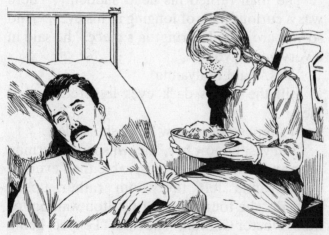

*"I shall lie in this bed forever."*

"Yes, and my Aunt Polly would agree with me," said Pollyanna.

"Aunt Polly?" said the man.

"She is Miss Polly Harrington. I live with her."

"Miss Polly Harrington!" he gasped, quite surprised. "You live with her?"

"Yes, I'm her niece."

The man fell absolutely silent, almost as if he had been stunned by what he had heard.

After a while Pollyanna said that perhaps she should go. "I hope you enjoy the jelly," she said, turning toward the door.

The man turned his head suddenly. There was a curious look of longing in his eyes. "And so you are Miss Harrington's niece," he said in a very gentle voice.

"Yes," said Pollyanna.

Still the man's dark eyes lingered on her face.

"I suppose you know her," she added.

"Oh yes, I know her," he whispered, turning over and looking more miserable than ever.

Pollyanna left the room rather upset. Outside, she found Doctor Chilton waiting for her. "Doctor Chilton," she said, "I expect being a doctor is one of the gladdest kinds of jobs."

The doctor turned in surprise. "Gladdest," he said. "I don't know about that. I see so much pain and suffering."

"But you're always helping people," said Pollyanna.

The doctor's eyes filled with tears. He was, in fact, a very lonely man. He lived by himself in a tiny apartment. Pollyanna's words had touched him like a loving hand.

"God bless you child," he said. "Every doctor could do with a tonic like you."

"And you should be glad," she said, "because you are different to all your patients. You are not ill."

The doctor nodded and smiled. "You do have a unique way of seeing everything, Pollyanna," he said.

# Chapter 13
## *Miss Polly in Love?*

A week later, Pollyanna found Miss Polly in her bedroom, doing her hair.

"Oh, please let me comb it for you," said the little girl. "I can do it a lot better than you."

"Don't be so foolish!" was the reply.

But before her aunt knew it, Pollyanna had the comb in her hand and was at work on her hair.

"Oh what pretty hair you have," she said. "And there's so much of it. You should show it off. I'm going to make you so pretty that people will just love to look at you."

Despite all her protests, Pollyanna managed to keep her aunt in front of the mirror until she was done.

When Miss Polly saw herself, her cheeks had flushed a pretty pink. She saw a face, not young it was true, but alive and quite beautiful. The eyes still sparkled. And Pollyanna's combing had indeed made her hair look very attractive.

*Miss Polly's cheeks had flushed a pretty pink.*

She was still looking thoughtfully at herself when Pollyanna dashed out of the room, only to return a few moments later with a rose she had picked from the garden. She pinned it carefully in Miss Polly's hair.

Pollyanna saw her aunt look into the mirror again and was sure tears appeared in her eyes.

That evening a message arrived from Mr. Pendleton. He wanted Pollyanna to call.

She was happy to go, and was most surprised when she was greeted with a smile.

"You must be a very forgiving person," he said. "Or else you wouldn't have come round to see me."

"I'm glad to come to see you," she said.

"But I was very rude to you when you found me with my broken leg. And I was so grumpy that I never really thanked you for the jelly."

Mr. Pendleton had a box at his bedside, containing many interesting things. He showed Pollyanna lots of the treasures he had collected on his travels abroad. She was fascinated. Later, he put the box down and spoke to her seriously.

"When I saw you the other day and learned who you were," he said, "you reminded me of something I have tried to forget for many years. But I'm not sure I want to forget it now. That's why I would love to see you whenever you can come over."

"I'd love to come," said Pollyanna, feeling so sorry for the man lying in the bed. But she was puzzled at what he might want to forget. She wasn't brave enough to ask him.

Later that evening Pollyanna told Nancy all that had happened at Mr. Pendleton's house.

"It's amazing," said Nancy. "He's normally so cross and angry—he never wants to talk to anyone."

"But he isn't cross and angry on the inside," insisted Pollyanna.

"Well, he's obviously taken to you, almost like a father," said Nancy. "And we always thought he disliked everyone."

"He told me that he was unhappy because I reminded him of something he wanted to forget," explained Pollyanna. "Then he changed his mind, I think, and wanted to remember. It was all very confusing."

"It sounds like one of those mysteries you read in books," said Nancy. "But I think I might just guess something about this mystery. Old Tom's known Miss Polly all her life and he told me that she fell in love once. And he

*The box contained many interesting things.*

said that the man was still living in the town. It seems to me that Mr. Pendleton and Miss Polly might have been in love once."

"But he said I reminded him of something he wanted to forget," said Pollyanna.

"Perhaps she broke his heart," said Nancy. "That's why it's painful for him to remember."

"But with both of them alone and sad," said Pollyanna, "you'd think they'd be glad to make things up and become friends again."

# Chapter 14
## *Sunshine Rainbows*

As the warm August days passed, Pollyanna frequently visited Mr. Pendleton. But she didn't think her visits were a great success. They didn't seem to make him any happier.

He talked quite a lot and he showed her many more of his treasures. But there always seemed something very sad about him. Pollyanna had thought about teaching him her game, but she hadn't seen a suitable occasion on which to introduce the subject.

Pollyanna was only eleven years old, but she understood many things beyond her age. And one of those was that she was sure Mr. Pendleton and Miss Polly had once loved each other dearly. Pollyanna desperately wanted to bring the pair together, and make their miserable and lonely lives happy.

One day she arrived at Mr. Pendleton's home and found him still in bed. His leg was taking a long while to mend. Then on his pillow she saw some sparkling patterns. She looked on in awe at the bright colors, dancing on the white linen.

"What is it?" she cried. "They are like baby rainbows! How can you have such a beautiful thing on your pillow?"

Mr. Pendleton pointed to the baubles of cut glass that he had asked the nurse to hang across his bedroom window, and explained how beams of sunlight touched it and splintered into all the different colors. "That's how the rainbow is formed," he said, "and there's not even a rain cloud in sight."

He saw how fascinated Pollyanna was with the rainbow and promised to make her one for her own bedroom window.

"How lovely," she said. "Perhaps I should really give it to Miss Polly. She needs some pretty rainbows in her life. I reckon she'd be glad of them for sure."

Mr. Pendleton laughed. "Well, from my remembrance of your aunt I think it would take more than a few rainbows to make her glad about some things."

At last Pollyanna had found her moment to introduce Mr. Pendleton to her game. She told him the whole thing, from the time her father

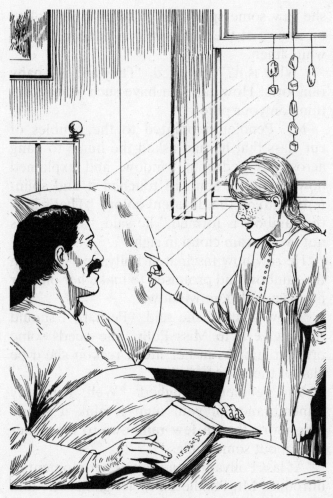

*"They are like baby rainbows!"*

first played it. When she got to the bit about being sent the crutches instead of the doll, he seemed to understand the game completely.

All the time she spoke, she watched the rainbows dancing around the room. "So you see," she said finally. "That's why I like the rainbows. They make me feel so very, very glad to be alive. So if the sun can play the game, then so can you."

Mr. Pendleton thought for a moment and then spoke. "Perhaps the most beautiful rainbow of them all is you," he said. "And I'm glad of that."

"No!" she said, shaking her head and pointing to the top of her nose. "The sun shines on me but it doesn't make beautiful rainbows. It just brings out my freckles. And that doesn't make me feel glad at all. I hate my freckles."

The man laughed again, and this time Pollyanna noticed that the laugh had sounded almost like a sob.

***

Mr. Pendleton wasn't the only person that that the young girl had come to like. There was Doctor Chilton, too. But in a strange way,

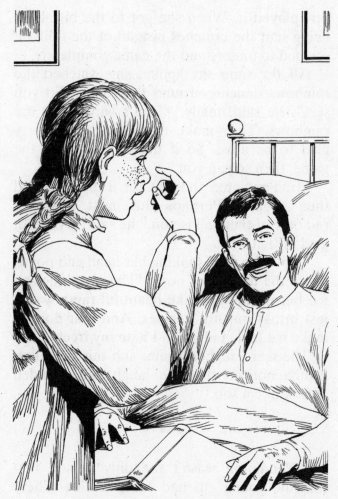

*Showing Mr. Pendleton her freckles.*

Miss Polly didn't seem to approve of her liking him.

One day when Miss Polly had a cold, Pollyanna suggested they should call Doctor Chilton. "I like him so much," she said.

"No!" said Miss Polly severely. "He is not our official doctor. He'll only make me worse. I don't want him anywhere near this house. Call Doctor Warren instead."

Pollyanna was very surprised at how her aunt had reacted to the doctor's name.

She began to wonder if Aunt Polly and the doctor had a shared past . . .

# Chapter 15
## *Mr. Pendleton Makes an Offer*

Pollyanna entered school that September. She soon settled in with all the other boys and girls in her class. School, in some ways, came as a surprise to Pollyanna; and Pollyanna, was in many ways, very much of a surprise to her school.

However, they were soon on the best of terms and to the delight of Aunt Polly, young Pollyanna declared that going to school was really living after all. But she did miss her regular visits to John Pendleton. She only saw him at weekends now.

Mr. Pendleton was also missing her. "See here, Pollyanna," he said one Saturday afternoon, "how would you like to come and live with me? I don't see much of you nowadays."

Pollyanna laughed. "You are a strange man," she said. "I thought you didn't like to have folks around."

He made a wry face. "Oh, but that was before you taught me your wonderful game.

*"How would you like to come and live with me?"*

Now I'm glad to be waited on hand and foot, and visited by people. And I'll soon be on my two feet again."

Pollyanna didn't believe him. "You aren't really glad at all for things," she said. "You just say you are. You don't play my game properly."

The man's face grew suddenly very serious. "That's why I want you to help me," he said. "I want you to help me play it by coming to live with me. I could adopt you."

"Mr. Pendleton," she replied solemnly. "You don't really mean that."

"But I do. I do. I want you to come," said the man.

"Mr. Pendleton, you know I can't," sighed Pollyanna. "I'm Aunt Polly's. I belong to Aunt Polly."

"She might let you go," he continued. "Would you come if she did?"

Pollyanna frowned in deep thought. "But Aunt Polly has been so good to me. And she took me in when I didn't have anyone."

His face looked gloomier than ever. "Pollyanna," he said, "many years ago I loved someone very much. I hoped to bring her to this house. I pictured how happy we would be together in our home."

"Yes, I understand," said Pollyanna, who was still convinced that he was talking about Aunt Polly.

"But I didn't bring her here," he continued. "Never mind why not. I just didn't—that's all. And ever since then this great gray pile of stone has been a house, but never a home. It takes a woman's hand and heart, or a child's presence, to make a home. And I have had neither. Now will you come, my dear?"

Pollyanna sprang to her feet, her face shining bright. "Mr. Pendleton, you mean that you wish you still had that woman's hand and heart after all this time?"

"Why, yes, Pollyanna," he said.

"Oh, I'm so glad," she said. "Then it's all right. Now you can take both of us, and everything will be lovely."

"Take you both?" said the man, with a puzzled look.

"Well of course," said Pollyanna. "Aunt Polly isn't won over yet, but I'm sure she could be. She's lonely. And then, of course, we could both come to live with you."

"Aunt Polly, come here?" he spluttered.

Pollyanna's eyes opened wider. "Would you rather go to live in her house?" she asked. "Of

91

*Pollyanna sprang to her feet.*

course, her house isn't as pretty as yours."

"Pollyanna, what are you talking about?" Mr. Pendleton asked her in a very gentle way.

"Why, about where we're going to live, of course," she said. "You said you wanted Aunt Polly's hand and heart to make a home."

A cry came from the man's throat. "For heaven's sake," he said, "say nothing about this. Who knows what trouble it could bring? You've got it all wrong, child."

# Chapter 16
## *A Shock for Pollyanna*

The next afternoon Pollyanna was on her way back from Sunday school when Doctor Chilton pulled up beside her in his horse and gig.

"I've got a message from Mr. Pendleton for you," he said. "He wants to see you. I'm heading out that way, so I can drop you off there."

"I guessed he might ask to see me today," she said, getting into the gig.

"I'm not sure it's entirely a good thing," he smiled, as they set off for John Pendleton's. "You seemed more to upset him than sooth him yesterday."

Pollyanna laughed. "Oh it wasn't truly me," she said. "It was more Aunt Polly."

"Your aunt!" he exclaimed.

"Yes and it's so exciting," she suddenly burst out. "It's just like a story, you know. I'm going to tell you even though he said not to mention it. But he wouldn't mind you knowing, of course. He meant not to mention it to her."

"Her?" asked the doctor.

"Yes. Aunt Polly. And, of course, he would want to tell her himself instead of me having to. What funny things lovers are."

"Lovers!" As the doctor said the word, the horse started violently, as if the hand that held the reins had given them a sharp jerk.

"Yes," nodded Pollyanna happily. "That's the story part. I didn't know it until Nancy told me. She said that Aunt Polly had been in love once many years ago and that she had quarreled with the person she loved. Nancy didn't know who it was at first. But we've found out now. It's Mr. Pendleton, you know."

The doctor suddenly looked sad. The hand holding the rein fell limply into his lap. "Oh, no. I didn't know," he said quietly.

"Yes, and I'm glad," said Pollyanna. "It's all come out lovely. Mr. Pendleton asked me to come and live with him, but of course I wouldn't leave Aunt Polly like that. She's been so good to me. But if he makes up his quarrel with my aunt now, everything will be all right. Aunt Polly and I will both go and live with him. Of course, my aunt doesn't know all this yet. I suppose that's why he wants to see me this afternoon."

*Setting off for John Pendleton's.*

The child's words had completely confused the doctor. He didn't understand what she was talking about. And as Pollyanna was about to discover later, Miss Polly had been in love once. But not with Mr. Pendleton.

Pollyanna found a very nervous Mr. Pendleton waiting for her.

"Pollyanna," he said. "I've been trying all night to puzzle out what you meant by all that yesterday . . . about my wanting your Aunt Polly's hand and heart. What did you mean?"

"Why, because you were both in love with each other once," said Pollyanna. "I was so glad you still felt the same way."

"In love . . . your Aunt Polly and I?" he said, with huge surprise.

"Nancy said you were in love," said Pollyanna.

The man gave a short little laugh. "Well, I'm afraid that Nancy got it wrong."

"Then you weren't in love with Aunt Polly?" said Pollyanna, her voice tragic with dismay.

"Never," he said firmly.

"Then it's not all coming out like the story in a book," she said disappointedly.

There was no answer. The man's eyes were moodily fixed on the window.

*"Then you weren't in love with Aunt Polly?"*

"Oh dear," said Pollyanna, bursting into
tears. "It was all going so smoothly. I would
have been so glad to have moved here with my
aunt."

"And won't you come now?" he asked.

"Of course not. I am Aunt Polly's," was the
reply.

The man, who seemed very disappointed,
looked Pollyanna closely in the eye. "You did
get half the story right," he said softly. "I was
in love once. But not with Aunt Polly . . . no,
it was your mother. And it was your mother's
hand and heart that I wanted all those years
ago. And it was she that you reminded me
of."

"My mother," whispered Pollyanna, quite
shaken by the confession.

"Yes. I hadn't meant to tell you, but perhaps
it's better after all."

Little Pollyanna, her eyes wide and frightened, gazed at Mr. Pendleton as he began his
story.

# Chapter 17

## *A Sad Story*

"I loved your mother," Mr. Pendleton began, "but she didn't love me. And after a time she married your father. I didn't know until then how much I loved her.

"I was heartbroken and that's why I have been such a cross, bad-tempered man, hiding away from people all the time. Then, one day, like one of those baubles that produced a rainbow, you danced into my life and colored my world with the dashes of purple, gold, and scarlet of your bright cheeriness.

"At first I didn't want to see you again because you reminded me of your mother. But things have just turned out differently. I became so fond of you I wanted to offer you a home. I still want to."

Pollyanna had been listening to every word. "But Mr. Pendleton," she said softly, "there's Aunt Polly."

"It's only since you came into my life that

*"I would give you everything, Pollyanna."*

I've learned to be even half-glad to be alive,"
he continued. "And if I had you for a daughter,
I would come fully alive once more. And I could
make you glad too. I would give you everything,
Pollyanna. I would use all my money, to the last
cent, to make you happy and glad."

Pollyanna looked shocked. "Why, Mr. Pendleton, as if I'd let you spend it on me. Besides,
Aunt Polly has been so good to me."

"Of course she has," interrupted Mr. Pendleton. "But does she want you as much as me?

I think she'd still prefer to live alone. She's always said so."

"I think she's learning to like having me in her house," said Pollyanna.

"I'll wager Miss Polly doesn't know how to be glad for anything," he said. "For her, life is about doing her duty. I will admit that we haven't been the best of friends over the years. But I do know her. And she isn't a glad sort of person. She doesn't know how to be. As for your coming to my house, you just ask her and see if she won't let you come."

Pollyanna rose to her feet with a heavy sigh. "All right, I'll ask her," she said. "Of course, I don't mean that I wouldn't like to live here with you but . . ."

There was a moment's silence, and then she went on. "Well, anyway, I'm glad I didn't tell her yesterday about how I thought you and she had fallen in love."

"Yes," said Mr. Pendleton, "I guess it's just as well you didn't mention it to her."

\*\*\*

The sky was darkening fast with what appeared to be an approaching thunderstorm when Polly-

*"Miss Polly sent me to find you."*

anna hurried down the hill from John Pendleton's house.

Halfway home she met Nancy. "Miss Polly sent me to find you," she said. "She was getting worried about you."

"Was she?" replied Pollyanna absent-mindedly, staring at the sky.

"Are you listening to me?" asked Nancy. "I said your aunt was worried about you."

"Oh sorry," she replied, still thinking of the question she had to ask Miss Polly.

"Yes, she often worries about you now," said Nancy. "She's become almost human since you arrived. She still thinks she's doing her duty to you, but she's learning to do it with affection."

Pollyanna wasn't so sure. "They do say she is a very dutiful woman."

"But she's changing," said Nancy.

"That's what I wanted to ask you, Nancy," she said. "Do you think Aunt Polly likes to have me here? Would she mind if I wasn't there?"

# Chapter 18
## *Pollyanna Has An Idea*

Nancy threw a shocked look at Pollyanna, as they continued to walk home. What had got into the girl? "Of course Miss Polly would mind if you weren't here," she finally said. "Didn't she send me to make sure you were safe and sound, just because there was a thunder cloud in the sky?

"Didn't she move you from the attic to a room beside hers? She has changed so much. There's the dog and the cat, too. She'd never have let them in the house before you came. Pollyanna, there ain't no telling how much your aunt would miss you if you weren't here."

A look of joy crossed Pollyanna's face. "Oh Nancy," she said. "I'm so glad. You don't know how glad that makes me, to think that Aunt Polly really wants me."

Later, she climbed the stairs to her room. Fluffy the cat was in her arms and Buffy the dog followed closely at her heels.

*Climbing the stairs to her room.*

"As if I'd leave Aunt Polly now," she said to them. "Of course I wouldn't! She likes me here. I could never leave."

But the task of telling John Pendleton wasn't an easy one. Pollyanna dreaded having to break the news to him. She had become very fond of Mr. Pendleton. She grieved that it was her mother who had broken his heart. But she also understood that part of the problem was that he felt sorry for himself.

The next morning as she got dressed, Pollyanna pictured Mr. Pendleton's huge house as it would be when his leg had mended. It would become empty again. The nurse would have gone. The doctor wouldn't call any more. The rooms would be silent.

Pollyanna's heart ached for him. Oh how she wished she could wave a magic wand and make him happy again. And it was at that very moment that she sprang to her feet with a cry of joy. A thought had just struck her!

After breakfast she hurried up the hill to John Pendleton's. He was pleased to see her; eager to know if Pollyanna had asked Aunt Polly if she could come and live with him.

"I didn't need to," she said. "I've found the answer myself."

*She saw the sadness in his face.*

"You mean you will come to share my house?" he asked.

"No," said Pollyanna, "but . . ."

Mr. Pendleton interrupted. "You aren't going to say no, are you?"

"I've got to stay with my aunt," she said. "I truly have. But I have found the answer."

"Tell me first what Aunt Polly said to you," he said.

"I didn't ask her," she said. "Nancy told me how much my aunt liked having me now. Aunt Polly wants me with her. She's beginning to be glad about all sorts of things. So I couldn't leave her now."

There was a long pause. At last he spoke. "Oh Pollyanna, I do understand," he said in a quiet and gentle voice. "I won't ask you again."

She saw the sadness in his face. "But you haven't heard my plan," she said excitedly. "There is something you can do. It's the gladdest thing I can think of. Truly it is."

"Not for me, Pollyanna," he said.

"Yes, Mr. Pendleton, for you! You said it yourself. You said that only a woman's hand or a child's presence could make a home. And I can get it for you. A child's presence . . . I can get that for you. Not me, but another one."

"As if I would have anyone but you," he replied. "And who would you be thinking about?"

"Jimmy Bean!"

"And who's he?" asked Mr. Pendleton.

"The child's presence you wanted," she said. "He so desperately needs a home. You'll make him so glad if you take him in."

"But he's not the one I want," said Mr. Pendleton.

"Do you mean you wouldn't take him?" she asked.

"I certainly do mean just that," he said.

"But he would be a lovely child's presence," faltered Pollyanna, who was almost crying now. "And you could never be lonely with Jimmy around."

# Chapter 19

## *Pollyanna Talks with Doctor Chilton*

It was while Pollyanna was talking to Mr. Pendleton about Jimmy Bean that she remembered Nancy talking about a skeleton he kept in his cupboard. She now mentioned this to Mr. Pendleton.

Suddenly the man threw back his head and started to laugh. He laughed very heartily indeed. Pollyanna still hadn't understood what a skeleton in a cupboard was.

"Oh Pollyanna," he said. "I expect you are right. I know a nice little boy would be far better for me than my skeleton. But the trouble is that we aren't always willing to make the exchange. We sometimes try and cling on to our skeletons. But I will listen to you. Tell me more about this boy."

And Pollyanna told him all she knew about Jimmy Bean.

Perhaps it was John Pendleton laughing at Pollyanna's mistaken idea about a skeleton in the cupboard that changed the atmosphere in the room. It had cleared the air.

Mr. Pendleton had lost his irritability and was much more relaxed. As Pollyanna spoke of Jimmy Bean, he opened his heart and allowed the sad story of the young boy to touch him.

When Pollyanna set off home that evening, her heart was filled with gladness. She carried with her an invitation for Jimmy Bean to visit Mr. Pendleton on the following Saturday.

"I'm so glad," she called out, as she waved goodbye to Mr. Pendleton. "I'm sure you'll

*Pollyanna's heart was filled with gladness.*

like him. I do so want Jimmy to have a real home and folks that care for him!"

Soon after leaving, Pollyanna saw Doctor Chilton standing outside his front door.

She had never seen his house before. "Is this your home?" she asked.

The doctor smiled a little sadly. "Yes," he said. "Such as it is. But it's a pretty poor apology for a home, Pollyanna. There are just rooms here; not a home."

Pollyanna nodded her head wisely. For one so young, her eyes glowed with a sympathetic understanding. "I know," she said, "it takes a woman's hand and heart, or a child's presence, to make a home."

"What?" said the doctor, surprised at such a statement. "Where did you hear that?"

"Mr. Pendleton told me about the woman's hand and heart, or the child's presence," she said. "Perhaps you should get a woman's hand and heart. Or maybe you'd take in Jimmy Bean. That is, if Mr. Pendleton doesn't want him."

Doctor Chilton laughed. "So Mr. Pendleton says it takes a woman's hand and heart, or a child to make a home, does he?" he asked.

"Yes," said Pollyanna. "And he says his

*"Perhaps you should get a woman's hand and heart."*

place is just a house rather than a home. So why don't you?"

"So why don't I what?" he asked.

"Get a woman's hand and heart," said Pollyanna, who just then remembered she had a matter to clear up. "By the by, I ought to tell you that it wasn't Aunt Polly who fell in love with Mr. Pendleton long ago. I made a mistake. So Aunt Polly and I will not be going to stay there. I hope you didn't tell anyone what I said."

"No. I didn't," said the doctor.

"And talking of love," said Pollyanna. "Why haven't you got a woman's hand and heart?"

There was a moment's silence before he answered. "They're not always to be had for the asking, little girl," he said.

"But you're a nice man," she insisted. "You could get one quite easily."

"Thank you for being so kind," said the doctor, laughing out aloud. "But it's not that easy to fall in love, and it can be painful."

"That sounds like you were once in love," replied Pollyanna, mischievously. "Did you find a woman's hand and heart?"

"Never you mind, my nosey little friend," he answered.

# Chapter 20
## *The Accident*

After Pollyanna left Doctor Chilton, she was
very surprised to see the local church minister,
the Reverend Paul Ford, sitting by the roadside with his head in his hands. At first she
thought he had been hurt, but that wasn't the
case. He had walked a little way out of town
to get some peace and quiet away from his
squabbling, back-biting, gossiping, and jealous
parishioners.

"What's the matter, Reverend?" asked Pollyanna. "Are you ill?"

"No, Miss Pollyanna," he replied. "I'm just
enjoying the peace and quiet of God's country
and trying to find it in myself to forgive some
rather ungodly parishioners."

"My father was a minister," said Pollyanna,
sitting down beside him. "He often took off to
escape his troublesome parishioners. He wrote
all his sermons in the peace and quiet of the
countryside."

"That's what I should do," he said. "I have so many problems that I can't think what to say in my Sunday sermon."

"Oh that's easy," said Pollyanna, "tell them about my 'glad' game."

The minister had heard all about Pollyanna's magical game. "What a wonderful idea," he said. "That might make my parishioners sit up and think."

The minister went home and wrote a sermon based on Pollyanna's game. On Sunday, it was a great success. And on the following Monday, he told Pollyanna how glad he was that he had bumped into her.

Unfortunately, Monday was also the day of Pollyanna's accident. She had been running home from school and dashing across the main road into town, when she was hit by a speeding motor car! The driver hadn't been able to stop his brand new machine in time, when Pollyanna had run in front of him.

Pollyanna was carried home unconscious. There she was tended to by a white-faced Aunt Polly and a weeping Nancy, while they waited for Doctor Warren to arrive.

Later, Nancy went out to tell Old Tom what had happened. "You only had to look at Miss

# The Accident

*"Tell them about my 'glad' game."*

Polly's face to see how much she loves that
girl," she said. "She might say she only took
that girl in for duty's sake. But those looks I
saw tell a different story. No one loves Pollyanna more than Miss Polly."

"How badly is Pollyanna hurt?" Old Tom
asked.

"There ain't no telling," sobbed Nancy.
"She's lying there as white as a sheet. She looked
dead to me. But Miss Polly said she wasn't. She
kept on listening to her heart and feeling her
pulse."

The doctor came. And the doctor left. There
was nothing he could do. There were possibly
some broken bones, but he couldn't tell which.
At least the cuts Pollyanna had suffered were
not deep. But he had spoken gravely about a
possible head or back injury.

"Time alone will tell," he'd said.

Night fell, and Pollyanna was still unconscious. Aunt Polly stayed by her bedside all
night, not closing her eyes once. She just stared
at Pollyanna and prayed. How she had come
to love that girl! Yet she still couldn't bring
herself to say it openly.

In the morning Pollyanna still had not
stirred, but her breathing seemed a little easier.

# The Accident

*There was nothing the doctor could do.*

Then at last, just before lunch, she opened her eyes and saw Aunt Polly at her bedside. "Is it time to get up?" she asked.

"No," said Aunt Polly. "Just rest for now. You've had an accident. An automobile hit you yesterday."

"I feel so odd," said Pollyanna. "My legs . . . I can't feel them at all."

With that, she closed her eyes again.

A trained nurse, Miss Hunt, arrived at the Harrington homestead to help Miss Polly and Nancy look after the little girl. Mr. Pendleton called by, and left some baubles to hang at her window, so she could see rainbows when she was awake. He was walking with crutches now, and could get about by himself again.

Pollyanna drifted in and out of consciousness for some time. Whenever she awoke, she always wanted to get up. She would get quite angry, especially when Nurse Hunt told her that she must stay in bed, rest, and take the pills that the doctor had ordered.

"Calm down, child," she said. "I only want to take care of you."

"But I don't want to be taken care of," replied Pollyanna. "I want to get up and go to school. Can I go tomorrow?"

"Tomorrow?" smiled the nurse. "I'm not sure we can let you out of here that soon. But you just swallow the pills and it won't be long before you can go."

"All right," said Pollyanna, somewhat doubtfully, "but I must go to school tomorrow. It's examination time."

Pollyanna did not go to school the next day, or for many days after that.

# Chapter 21

## *A Visit from Mr. Pendleton*

It was a week before Pollyanna fully regained consciousness, and even then she still couldn't move her legs. "Am I still sick?" she asked Aunt Polly.

"You aren't sick at all," replied her aunt. "But you are still injured."

"Oh I'm so glad I'm just hurt and not sick," she said. "I'm glad it's not smallpox that ails me. That would be worse than freckles. And I'm glad it's not whooping cough. I've had that and it's horrid. And I'm glad it's not measles because that's catching."

Aunt Polly smiled. "You seem to be glad for a good many things, my dear," she said.

"I am," said Pollyanna. "I've been thinking of them, lots of them, all the time. I've been looking up at the rainbows that Mr. Pendleton gave me. I love those shiny baubles and the colors they make. But mostly I'm glad that just now you called me 'my dear'."

To be truthful, Aunt Polly hadn't been aware she had used the words. They had been said instinctively rather than out of duty.

"It's only since I've been hurt that you have called me that," said Pollyanna. "And I love it. Please don't stop now. It makes me feel as though I belong to you, and you belong to me. And that's lots of things to be glad about, isn't it. I'm so glad you belong to me."

It was all too much for Miss Polly. Her eyes were full of tears and she had to turn away and hurry out of the room.

That afternoon Mr. Pendleton called on Miss Polly, to see how Pollyanna was.

A flash of pain crossed the woman's face, when he asked after the child.

"I can't tell you how she is," she said. "I wish I could."

"You mean you don't know?"

"That's the truth," she replied.

"But . . . the doctor?"

"Doctor Warren is not sure," she said, "but he's contacting a New York specialist for advice. He's hoping the man will give her a consultation."

"But what were the injuries?" asked Mr. Pendleton.

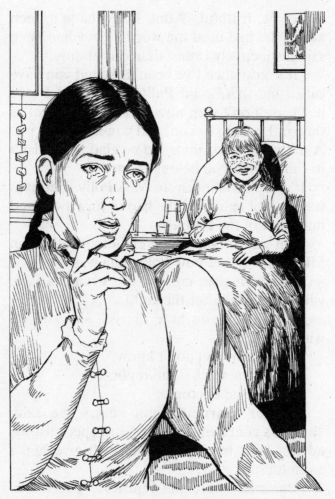

*Miss Polly's eyes were full of tears.*

"A slight cut on her head and one or two bruises," said Miss Polly, "but the real problem, I believe, is an injury to her spine. She seems to be paralyzed from the hips down."

A sad cry came from Mr. Pendleton. "Oh my goodness," he said. "How is Pollyanna taking it?"

"She knows she can't move her legs," replied Miss Polly, "but she believes her legs are broken. She says she's glad it's only broken legs rather than some lifelong injury. But the truth is that she is probably paralyzed for life."

Through the blur of his own tears, Mr. Pendleton saw how terribly drawn Miss Polly's face had become. He dearly wanted to say something that would cheer her. His thoughts went back to how Pollyanna had refused his offer of a home. "Do you know," he said, "that several times I offered Pollyanna a home with me. I wanted to adopt her and make her my heir."

Miss Polly was surprised at the news.

"I am very fond of Pollyanna," he continued. "I am fond of her for both her own sake and her late mother's."

"What did the girl say when you asked her?" said Miss Polly, hesitantly.

*"Pollyanna would not leave you."*

"Pollyanna would not leave you," he said. "She said you'd been so good to her. She wanted to stay with you . . . and even more importantly, she thought that you wanted her to stay."

Mr. Pendleton left soon after.

The next day Miss Polly spoke to Pollyanna about another doctor coming to see her.

"Who, Doctor Chilton?" she cried with happiness. "I'm so fond of him. I've always wished he would come instead of Doctor Warren."

"No," said Miss Polly. "This doctor is a specialist from New York. He knows an awful lot about the sort of injuries you have."

"I don't believe he knows half as much as Doctor Chilton," Pollyanna said.

"Oh, I'm sure he does," Miss Polly replied.

"But Doctor Chilton mended Mr. Pendleton's leg," Pollyanna protested. "So surely he can mend my legs."

Miss Polly was so distressed. She couldn't bear to tell the child the truth. So she decided to be her usual stern self. "It's for your own good. And believe me, Doctor Chilton does not know as much as the New York gentleman."

Pollyanna still looked unconvinced.

# Chapter 22
## *Doctor Mead's Visit*

In the days that followed, Aunt Polly did everything to keep Pollyanna cheered up.

Out in the garden, Nancy chatted with Old Tom, keeping him up to date with everything that was happening.

"Do you know," she said one day, "a few weeks ago Miss Polly would have screamed blue murder if Fluffy and Buffy had been seen in a bedroom. Now she lets them tumble all over Pollyanna's bed.

"And Miss Polly spends every moment hanging around, waiting to do something for that blessed lamb. And each time she goes into the child's bedroom, she taps those little glass danglers so Pollyanna can see the rainbows."

"It's good she's got someone to care for," said wise Old Tom. "She hasn't got so much time to think about herself now."

"The other day Pollyanna directed the nurse to do Miss Polly's hair with curls and a more

*Chatting with Old Tom in the garden.*

modern style," laughed Nancy. "Miss Polly looked years younger and very attractive."

"I told you she was attractive when she was young," said Old Tom. "There's no reason why she can't be attractive again."

"So come on Tom," said Nancy. "Surely you can tell me now who Miss Polly was once in love with."

"You won't find out from me," he said, laughing.

"You're an old devil, Tom," she said, "but I will find out."

"I'm sure you will," he smiled.

The talk turned to how Pollyanna was. And Old Tom told Nancy a story about the little girl and her game.

"She heard me growling one day about my aching bones and being all bent up and crooked," he said.

"I wouldn't think she could find anything in that to be glad about," said Nancy.

"Oh, yes she did," laughed Old Tom. "She said I should be glad that I didn't have to stoop down so far to do the weeding because I was already bent part of the way down!"

Nancy laughed. "Do you know something," she said. "It's strange. But Pollyanna has got half the people in the area playing her game—even the minister. But there is one person I don't think she has ever tried it on."

"And who's that?" asked Old Tom.

"Why, Miss Polly, of course," she replied.

"And why not?" asked Old Tom.

"Apparently," said Nancy, "it's because it was a game invented by Pollyanna's father. When she first came here she kept talking about her father. Miss Polly got a bit angry and told her to stop talking so much about him. That's the reason."

Old Tom sighed, and shook his head sadly.

\*\*\*

At last Doctor Mead, the specialist from New York, arrived. He was a tall, broad-shouldered man with kind gray eyes and a cheerful smile. He shook Pollyanna's hand when they were introduced.

Pollyanna liked him immediately. "You look exactly like my own doctor," she said.

"What? Like Doctor Warren?" he answered.

"Oh no!" she cried. "Doctor Warren is Aunt Polly's doctor. My doctor is Doctor Chilton."

131

*At last Doctor Mead arrived.*

Doctor Mead was a little puzzled that a young girl and the aunt she was living with should each have their own doctor.

"Yes," said Pollyanna. "I wanted my doctor to come and see me, but Aunt Polly wanted you. She said you knew more about broken legs than Doctor Chilton. And of course, if you do, I can be glad for that too. Do you know more about broken legs than Doctor Chilton?"

For a moment, the doctor didn't know what to say. He knew the seriousness of Pollyanna's injuries and he also knew that the girl thought her legs were broken.

"Only time will tell, young lady," he said at last.

Doctor Mead spent an hour examining Pollyanna. Then he took Aunt Polly out of the room. He wanted to talk to her privately. He closed the bedroom door but while he was talking to Aunt Polly, Fluffy the cat climbed the stairs, leapt up at the door latch, and opened it again.

The happy cat flew onto Pollyanna's bed, purring with joy. But Pollyanna wasn't paying attention to him. She could now overhear through the open door what the doctor was saying to Aunt Polly!

133

# Chapter 23
## *Terrible News*

Outside the open bedroom door, the doctor, the nurse, and Miss Polly stood talking.

"Not that! Doctor, not that!" cried Miss Polly. "You don't mean the child will never walk again!"

It was all confusion then. First, from the bedroom came Pollyanna's terrified call. "Aunt Polly! Aunt Polly!"

Then Miss Polly, seeing the open door, realized that her words had been overheard. She gave a moan and for the first time in her life fainted dead away, falling straight into the arms of Doctor Mead.

"Pollyanna must have heard," said the nurse, stumbling toward the door.

Inside, the nurse found the purring cat on the bed and a white-faced, wild-eyed little girl.

"Nurse, please I want Aunt Polly," said Pollyanna, in a quavering voice. "I want her right away. Quick. Please!"

*A white-faced, wild-eyed little girl.*

"I'll get her in a moment," answered Nurse Hunt. "She can't come just for the minute, dear. What is it? Can I get you something?"

Pollyanna shook her head. "I want to know what she said. Did you hear her? It was Aunt Polly. She said something. I want her to tell me it isn't true."

The nurse tried to speak but no words came. Something in her face frightened Pollyanna even more. She began to cry.

"Did you hear it?" she sobbed. "Is it true? Tell me it isn't. Does it mean I'll never walk again?"

"There, there, dear," murmured the nurse. "Don't cry. I'm not sure what the doctor was saying. Perhaps he doesn't really know. Perhaps he's mistaken. There are lots of things that could happen, you know."

"But Aunt Polly said he did know. She said he knew more than anybody else about what was wrong with me."

"Yes. Yes. I know dear," said the nurse. "But all doctors make mistakes sometimes. Just don't think about it any more. Please don't, dear."

Pollyanna flung out her arms wildly. "But I can't help thinking about it," she wailed. "It's all there is to think about. How will I get to school? How will I get to see Mr. Pendleton?"

Pollyanna caught her breath for a moment. Suddenly, she stopped and looked up, a new terror in her eyes. "Why," she said, "if I can't walk, how am I ever going to be glad about anything?"

The nurse did not know Pollyanna's game, but she did know the young girl had to be calmed down. She went and got a glass of water, into which she put a pill. Obediently, Pollyanna took the medicine. She did calm down a little. Then she spoke again, this time in a very quiet voice.

"I know Father used to say that there was always something about everything that might be worse. But I reckon nobody ever told him that he would never walk again. I don't see how there can be anything worse than that, do you, nurse?"

Nurse Hunt did not reply. She could not trust herself to speak just then.

\*\*\*

Nancy was sent to tell John Pendleton of Doctor Mead's verdict. "It's bad news," she said.

*Pollyanna took the medicine.*

"Tell me the worst," he answered.

"She won't walk again. The doctor says she'll never walk again. Never!"

For a moment, there was absolute silence. Then the man spoke in a voice shaking with emotion. "Poor little girl. Poor little girl!"

Nancy glanced at him. She had never ever expected to see such emotion coming from a person she had always thought of as stern and unemotional.

"It's so cruel," he said. "Never to dance in the sunshine again. Never to dance with her rainbows."

There was another silence and then he asked another question. "She herself doesn't know yet, of course, does she?"

"But she does, sir," replied Nancy. "And that's what makes it all the harder."

# Chapter 24

## *A Town Is Sad*

"Drat that cat!" cried Nancy as she explained to John Pendleton what had happened. "The cat pushed the door open and Pollyanna heard the doctor and Miss Polly talking."

"I feel so sorry for her," sighed the man again.

"Yes, sir," said Nancy. "She keeps thinking of all the things she'll never do again. She can't seem to be glad about anything. And that's not like her at all. Do you know about her game, sir?"

"I certainly do," he replied. "She told me all about that."

"Well, it's just so sad," said Nancy, a quaver in her voice. "She just can't play it any more and that worries her. She just can't think of a thing to be glad about."

"Well, why should she?" said Mr. Pendleton, almost savagely. He was so angry at the tragic news.

*Mr. Pendleton was so angry.*

"I reminded Pollyanna that she always saw something to be glad about," continued Nancy. "But the poor little lamb just cries and says it doesn't seem the same somehow. She says it's easy to tell people who have been invalids all their lives how to be glad. But then she says it's not the same when you're the life-long invalid yourself."

Nancy paused, but Mr. Pendleton didn't speak. He sat with his hands over his eyes.

"Then I reminded her," continued Nancy, "that she always said in the past that the game was all the nicer to play when it was hard. She always said the bigger the problem, the better the game. But now she says that's different, too."

Before Nancy left for home, she had one more question for Mr. Pendleton. "Sir, I don't suppose I could take Miss Pollyanna some good news, could I?"

"And what would that be?" he asked.

"Can I tell her you've seen Jimmy Bean, sir? Pollyanna does worry about the boy. And I know you were going to see him. She cares so much about that boy and him finding a home."

"I haven't yet," said John Pendleton. "But

I hope I will be able to give Pollyanna some good news soon."

It didn't take long for the entire town of Beldingsfield to hear that Pollyanna would never walk again. And never had a town been in such shock. Everybody now knew the little freckled girl who always wore a happy smile of greeting. And almost everybody knew the special game she played.

To think that never again would that smiling face be seen on their streets! It seemed to the townsfolk that what had happened was unbelievably cruel.

*Never had a town been in such shock.*

In kitchens and sitting rooms, and over backyard fences, women talked of it and wept openly. On street corners and in stores, men talked and wept—though not so openly.

And neither the talking nor the weeping grew less when, fast on the heels of the tragic news, they heard something else; something that was almost worse.

Little Pollyanna, they heard, could no longer play the game. She could see nothing to be glad about.

# Chapter 25
## *A Child's Presence*

A few days later, Mr. Pendleton came to visit again. He came without his crutches as his leg was now completely healed. "Can anything be done?" he asked Miss Polly.

"Doctor Mead holds no hope at all," she replied.

Miss Polly was quite shaken to see tears in Mr. Pendleton's eyes.

"I don't think it is wise for me to see Pollyanna just yet," he said. "The fact that I can walk again and she never will might make her even more upset. But I have a message for her. Tell her I have seen Jimmy Bean and he's going to be my boy from now on. I thought the news that I'm adopting him might just make her glad."

For a moment, Miss Polly lost her usual self-control and reserve. "You will adopt Jimmy Bean!" she gasped.

"Yes," he replied. "I think Pollyanna will

understand. You will tell her that I thought the news would make her glad."

"Why, of course," she said.

"Thank you," said John Pendleton, as he turned to leave.

In the middle of the floor, Miss Polly stood silent and amazed, staring at the man now walking away down the garden path. She could hardly believe what she had just heard. John Pendleton, adopt Jimmy Bean? John Pendleton, wealthy, independent, sad, miserly, and supremely selfish, to adopt a boy? And such a poor little boy, too!

Feeling somewhat dazed, Miss Polly went upstairs to Pollyanna's room. "Pollyanna," she said, "I have just had a message for you from Mr. Pendleton. He says to tell you that he has taken in Jimmy Bean to be his little boy. He is going to adopt him. He said he thought you would be glad to know it."

Pollyanna's pale face flamed into sudden joy for the first time in days.

"Glad? Glad?" she smiled. "Well, I reckon I am glad. Oh, Aunt Polly, I've so wanted to find a place for Jimmy. And Mr. Pendleton's is such a fine place for him. And I'm glad for Mr. Pendleton too. You see, now he'll have the

*John Pendleton, adopt Jimmy Bean?*

child's presence that I always talk about. He once said that only a woman's hand and heart, or a child's presence could make a real home. And now he's got it . . . the child's presence."

"Oh, I see!" exclaimed Miss Polly.

But Pollyanna hadn't finished. "And Doctor Chilton says so too," she said. "He is sure it takes a woman's hand and heart, or a child's presence, to make a home."

"How do you know that?" asked Miss Polly, taking special notice of what Pollyanna had said.

"He told me one day," she replied. "He said he didn't live in a home. It was just rooms he lived in."

Miss Polly did not answer. She was staring wistfully out of the window.

"So I asked Doctor Chilton why he didn't get a woman's hand and heart, or a child's presence. Then he could have a home too," continued Pollyanna.

"What did he say?" asked Miss Polly, turning back to her niece, suddenly very interested.

"He didn't say anything for a while," said Pollyanna. "Then he said it wasn't that easy to find such things. He said you couldn't always get that thing just by asking."

*Staring wistfully out of the window.*

A brief silence fell over the bedroom. Miss Polly's moist eyes had turned back to the window.

Pollyanna sighed. "But Doctor Chilton does want a home, I know. And I wish he could have one."

"And how do you know?" asked Aunt Polly.

"Because on another day, he said something else. He said it very quietly, but I heard him say it. He said he'd give the world for a woman's hand and heart."

Miss Polly didn't answer. She was staring sadly out of the window again—in the direction of the good doctor's house.

# Chapter 26
## *Visitors*

Over the next few days, Miss Polly found her homestead besieged with well-wishers from Beldingsfield. Some she knew, others were total strangers. Some came in and stayed for a few minutes. Others brought presents. But they all inquired anxiously about Pollyanna's condition, and left messages wishing her well.

First there was Millie Snow. "You don't know me," she said to Miss Polly, "but Pollyanna produced a miracle in our house. She taught my mother to play the game."

"What game?" said Miss Polly, who quite extraordinarily was one of the few people in the area not to know about the game.

"You must know Pollyanna's game," she replied. "She used it to help my mother. She always pretended to be sick and she'd never get out of bed. And she always bemoaned her lot, saying how unfortunate she was. Then Pollyanna came in and taught her the game.

"My mother came to see how glad she should be for so many things. She's a new woman, thanks to Pollyanna. So please give her our best wishes for a speedy recovery."

Then came Widow Benton. After she lost her husband, she became the unhappiest woman in town. She certainly became the dowdiest dresser, too.

"Pollyanna taught me to count my blessings with her game," she told an increasingly baffled Miss Polly. "She also told me I must dress prettily in memory of my husband. Will you send her my love and tell her I was wearing a bright red dress today?"

A third caller was Mrs. Tarbell. "I'm a stranger to you, Miss Polly," she said, "but not to your niece. My daughter died last year and I've been staying in town for my health and taking long walks every day. I met Pollyanna on one of those walks and she cheered me up.

"Pollyanna's smile reminded me of my daughter. She taught me to be glad for the time I had enjoyed with my daughter while she was alive. You can't imagine how much joy your niece has brought to me. Just tell her how glad I am now, but how sad I was to hear about her accident."

*Besieged with well-wishers from Beldingsfield.*

Miss Polly was left quite stunned to find out how Pollyanna had helped so many people. She was also much puzzled by talk of the "game".

Later that same week a Mrs. Payson visited. "I've just heard the news," she said. "I tell you, I love that child of yours so much that I would happily give up my two legs for her. She'd do more good trotting around on them in one hour than I could do in a hundred years. But never mind that. Legs ain't always given to the ones who can make best use of them."

"It's very kind of you to say so," said Miss Polly. "But how do you know my niece?"

"We fell on hard times recently," she said. "Me and my husband were close to divorce. The kids would have gone into a home. But Pollyanna came and spent many hours talking with us and our children.

"She made us see how glad we should be with our lot. I know she can't walk any more, but just tell her from us that we are just glad we ever met her. It was the game. She helped with the game."

As soon as Mrs. Payson left, Miss Polly hurried to have a talk with Nancy.

"Nancy!" she said quite sharply. "In the last few days I've had a succession of people I hardly know knocking at my door and wanting

*"Pollyanna taught me to count my blessings."*

to thank Pollyanna. Now tell me. Everyone in town seems to know what Pollyanna's game is except me. And they all seem to be playing it, too. Just tell me. What is this game?"

To Miss Polly's surprise, Nancy burst into tears. "It's just that since she arrived," she sobbed, "that blessed child has been making the whole town glad, and now that Pollyanna has had such bad luck, they're trying to make her a little glad too by coming around to ask after her."

*Nancy burst into tears.*

"Glad of what?" snapped Miss Polly.

"Just glad! That's the game."

Miss Polly actually stamped her foot in irritation. "There you go like the rest," she shouted. "What game?"

At last Nancy told her all about the story of how the crutches had arrived instead of a doll, and how Pollyanna's father had taught her that there was always something to be glad about.

Miss Polly couldn't believe it. "How can you ever be glad of crutches?" she demanded to know.

"Simple," said Nancy. "In Pollyanna's case, she could be glad she didn't need them! And believe me, if you try and find something to be glad about in a nasty situation, you will find it.

"Pollyanna made me glad about a lot of things. She even made me glad about Monday mornings. She said I should be glad when Monday morning came because it would be a whole week before the next one!"

Miss Polly was laughing now. She finally understood the game. The one thing that Aunt Polly didn't understand was why Pollyanna had never taught her to play it.

# Chapter 27
## *Miss Polly Learns to Play the Game*

"Nancy," repeated Miss Polly. "Tell me why everyone else in town knows about this game and I don't!"

Nancy answered in the briefest way possible. "It was a game taught to Pollyanna by her father. When she arrived here, the first thing you told her was that you didn't want to hear her talking about her father. She took you at your word."

Miss Polly bit her lip.

Nancy went on. "The dear little girl wanted to play the game with you from the very beginning, but she couldn't after what you said. So she started playing it with me."

"Well," choked Miss Polly through a veil of tears, "I know someone who'll play the game with her now!"

She sped through the kitchen and rushed straight upstairs to Pollyanna's bedroom.

"My dear little girl," she said. "You've had even more callers today wishing you well. Widow Benton was one of the latest. She told me to tell you that she was wearing a bright red dress today."

"That makes me glad," replied Pollyanna. "I must go and see her to thank her."

She suddenly stopped. "Oh why can't I remember that my legs don't go anywhere any longer? I won't ever go up to see Widow Benton again. Or Milly Snow, Mrs. Payson, or Mrs. Tarbell again. And so many others. They made me glad because I could help them."

Miss Polly sat down on the side of the bed. "I know why you didn't play the game with me. Nancy explained it was all to do with what I said about not letting you talk about your father. But I can play the game with you now."

"Oh Aunt Polly," cried Pollyanna. "I'm so glad. I really wanted to play the game with you more than almost anyone else."

"It's time I did," laughed Miss Polly through the tears. "The whole town is playing the game. And the whole town is happier . . . and all because of one little girl who taught the people a new game and how to play it."

*"I can play the game with you now."*

Pollyanna clapped her hands. "I'm so glad," she cried.

Then suddenly a wonderful light lit up her face. "Why, Aunt Polly," she said. "There is something I can be glad about in all of this. I can be glad that I once had legs that worked. If I hadn't had them, I couldn't have met all those people and made them glad."

\*\*\*

One by one the short winter days came and went. But they were not short for Pollyanna. They were long and sometimes full of pain. Yet she turned a cheerful face to whatever came. Was she not bound to play her own game if her aunt had promised to play it too? And Miss Polly now found so many things to be glad about.

Now Pollyanna was receiving guests. John Pendleton was a regular caller. So was Jimmy Bean. Jimmy told Pollyanna what a lovely home he had now. And Mr. Pendleton was just glad that by adopting Jimmy, he had created a real home and no longer lived in a house with rooms.

The winter passed and spring arrived. Pollyanna's condition hadn't improved. Doctor Mead's worst fears seemed to have been

161

*Now Pollyanna was receiving guests.*

realized. It was at this time that Doctor Chilton went to see John Pendleton at his home.

"John," he said. "I need your help. I want to examine Pollyanna."

"But surely you can," replied John.

"You know perfectly well that I have not been in the Harrington homestead for fifteen years."

John Pendleton did know. He knew that long ago Miss Polly had fallen in love with Doctor Chilton but that something had happened. There had been arguments between them.

"What did you quarrel about?" he asked. "I never did know."

"What's any lovers' argument about?" he replied. "It was nothing special, but then pride got in the way. She told me she wouldn't forgive me unless I apologized."

"So your pride got the better of you and you never did go back," said John Pendleton.

"You're right," he said. "I have never entered the house since. But now I must swallow my pride. I must enter that house. I must see that little girl. It is possibly a matter of life or death. It will mean, I honestly believe, that Pollyanna may walk again!"

# Chapter 28

## *Doctor Chilton and Miss Polly*

"Walk! Walk! What do you mean?" exclaimed John Pendleton.

"It's just that from what I hear," Doctor Chilton replied, "Pollyanna's case is very similar to one that a doctor friend of mine has just helped. However, I desperately need to see the girl first, to see if I can help. But, as you know, Miss Polly won't hear of it. She is too proud to forgive me."

"You must see her," said John Pendleton. "A way must be found!"

"But how?" asked the doctor.

The two men weren't to know that Jimmy Bean had been listening to their conversation. He had heard every word.

"By jinks!" he whispered to himself. "I know a way. And I'm going to do it."

Jimmy crept out of the house and ran as if

his life depended on it. He didn't stop until he reached the Harrington homestead. Nancy saw him coming and met him at the door.

"I must see Miss Polly!" he said.

"Are you sure you don't mean Miss Pollyanna?" asked Nancy.

"No. It must be Miss Polly," he insisted.

Nancy hurried off and found Miss Polly. A few minutes later she appeared.

"What can I do for you, my boy?" she asked.

"Ma'am," began Jimmy, "I suppose it's a dreadful thing I'm doing and what I'm a-saying. But I can't help it. It's for Pollyanna. And I'd walk over hot coals for her. She helped me, so I want to help her.

"You would too if you thought there was a chance of Pollyanna walkin' again. And that's why I'm here. It sounds rude, but I have to say that it's just pride between you and Doctor Chilton that may lose Pollyanna the chance to walk again."

"What on earth are you talking about?" Miss Polly wanted to know. "Now slow down and tell me exactly what you want to say."

"I overheard Doctor Chilton and Mr. Pendleton talking," he began. "And the doctor said that he knew some other doctor who might know how to cure Pollyanna. But the doctor says that you wouldn't let him in the house for some reason or other ... something to do with you being in love with him once. He said it was only pride that kept the two of you apart. And that's why you wouldn't let him in your house."

Miss Polly staggered onto a seat. "Never mind all that stuff," she said. "What about this other doctor, Jimmy, the one who might know a cure."

"I don't know who he was," replied Jimmy. "They didn't say. All Mr. Pendleton said after that was that he had to find a way to get you to let Doctor Chilton examine Pollyanna. That's why I came round. You must let him in!"

"Of course, he can come to examine Polly-anna," said Miss Polly. "He must come if there is any chance of helping her. You've been a good boy, Jimmy. Now run home immediately and tell him to come this very minute. And tell him this, too. I'm not as proud as I used to be. And I'm glad of it!"

Jimmy raced away, a huge grin on his face. At last he could repay the kindness that Pol-lyanna had shown to him. And he was glad of that.

*"I must see Miss Polly!"*

That same evening Doctor Chilton arrived at the Harrington homestead and was shown in to see Pollyanna.

"Oh Doctor Chilton," she cried on seeing him. "How glad I am to see you!"

Miss Polly appeared. "I am sorry, Pollyanna, that I wouldn't let Doctor Chilton see you before," she said. "And I hope it's not too late now."

The doctor examined Pollyanna closely. He lifted her legs up and down, pressed this and that, and generally examined every inch of her.

Then he smiled. "I want Pollyanna to see this doctor friend of mine. I am convinced he can help. I shall arrange for her to go and see him next week."

There was one last thing he wanted to say to Pollyanna. "I happen to know now that one of the gladdest jobs you ever did has been done today."

Pollyanna smiled knowingly, but Miss Polly didn't understand his words.

That evening, after the doctor had left, Miss Polly and Pollyanna were left alone to talk.

"Pollyanna," said Miss Polly, putting her arms around the girl, "I'm going to tell you a secret."

*Doctor Chilton arrived.*

"You don't need to tell me," she said. "I can guess."

"How can you?" asked her aunt.

"Something told me a long time ago that you were the woman's hand and heart that Doctor Chilton wanted," she said. "And when he said today that I had done one of my gladdest jobs, I knew what he meant. He was saying that somehow I had brought you and him together again. It makes me so glad. Why, Aunt Polly, I'm so glad that I don't even mind that my legs don't work."

"Oh, my darling girl," said Miss Polly. "I'm going to tell you a few things that make me glad. The first is that you have brought Doctor Chilton and me together again. The second is that I'm sure Doctor Chilton will continue to be a marvelous sort of uncle to you. The third is the most important thing of all. Next week, you're going to take a long journey to see Doctor Chilton's friend the doctor. And he's going to see what he can do for you!"

# Chapter 29
## *A Letter from Pollyanna*

Pollyanna did go to see Doctor Chilton's friend. She had to stay with the doctor for some time, but slowly, very slowly, she was getting better. Almost a year later, a letter addressed to Aunt Polly, Nancy, Old Tom, Doctor Chilton, Mr. Pendleton, and Jimmy Bean arrived at the Harrington homestead.

*Dear All,*
*Oh, I can. I can. I can walk! I did today. All the way from my bed to the window. It was six steps in all. My, how good it was to be on my legs again!*

*All the doctors stood around and smiled, and all the nurses cried. I don't see why they cried. I only wanted to sing, shout, and yell! Oh! Oh! Oh! Just think I can walk . . . walk . . . walk!*

*It's been worth spending ten months here. And how wonderful it was not to miss Aunt*

*Polly's wedding. Wasn't that just like you, dear Aunt, to come all the way here to get married to Doctor Chilton right beside my bed? You always think of the gladdest things now.*

*Pretty soon, they say, I shall be coming home. I will gladly walk the whole way, I promise. I don't think I will ever want to ride anywhere any more. I shall be just so glad to walk everywhere again. Oh, I'm so glad. I'm glad for everything. Why I'm glad now I lost my legs for a while, for you never know how perfectly lovely legs are till you haven't got them.*

*I'm going to walk eight steps tomorrow. Then more and more each day until you see me walking up the drive to the Harrington homestead.*

*With heaps of love to everybody,*
*Pollyanna.*

*"Pretty soon, they say, I shall be coming home."*

*The End*